Gordon
Dream

Illustrated by Peter Lawson
Series Editor: Teresa Wilson

Thomas the Tank Engine & Friends

A BRITT ALLCROFT COMPANY PRODUCTION

Based on The Railway Series by The Rev W Awdry

© Gullane (Thomas) LLC 2003

Published in Great Britain in 2003 by Egmont Books Limited,
239 Kensington High Street, London, W8 6SA
Printed in China
ISBN 0 7498 5751 X

10 9 8 7 6 5 4 3 2 1

Educational consultant: Nicola Morgan, literacy expert and author of over 60 early learning books.

It was the middle of the night.

The trains were sleeping.

But Gordon was having
a bad dream.

The door to his shed looked much too narrow.

I can't fit through that door, he thought.

Someone will have to make the door wider.

The tracks looked much too wide.

My wheels can't fit on those
wide tracks, he thought.

Someone will have to make
the tracks narrower.

The truck looked much too heavy.

I can't pull that truck, he thought.

It looks much too heavy.

Someone will have to make it lighter.

The signal looked much too big.

I will never get past that,
he thought.

Someone will have to make it smaller.

11

The bridge looked much too small.

I will never fit under that bridge,
he thought.

I am much too tall.

My funnel will fall off!

The hill looked much too high.

I can't go as high as that, he thought.

Someone else will have to go.

In the morning, The Fat Controller arrived.

"I want you to take these trucks to the top of the hill," he said to Gordon.

"I can't," said Gordon.

"The hill is too high,
the trucks are too heavy,
the bridge is too small
AND the track is too wide
for my wheels."

The Fat Controller laughed.

"You've had a bad dream," he said.

"But it's not real!
You're the biggest, strongest engine I know!"

Gordon was very pleased.

"I'm the fastest engine too," he said.

He raced off towards the hill, pulling the trucks behind him.

"Poop, poop!" he cried, all the way to the top of the hill.